Dream Wolf

"We did not think of the great open plains, the beautiful rolling hills and the winding streams with tangled growth, as 'wild.' Only to the white man was nature a 'wilderness' and only to him was the land 'infested' with 'wild' animals and 'savage' people. To us it was tame. Earth was bountiful and we were surrounded with the blessings of the Great Mystery."
—*Chief Standing Bear of the Lakota*

Dream Wolf

Story and illustrations by Paul Goble

Bradbury Press   New York

Indian people have wonderful stories of wolves (and other animals) who helped women and children when they were lost or in danger; stories of men who were wounded, far from home and help, whom the wolves fed until they recovered.

For centuries Indian people relied upon their dogs to help them. This close relationship extended to the wolves. We, too, love our dogs, and yet we seem unable to see the same expressions in the faces of wolves. We have driven them from nearly every part of North America, and where they still live they are fearful of us. Where the wolf no longer roams he is missed by everything in nature. We feel his loss; Creation is incomplete.

For Mrs. Anna

The full-color illustrations have been reproduced from the original artwork for this new edition of *The Friendly Wolf*, co-authored by Paul and Dorothy Goble, with illustrations by Paul Goble, which was originally published in 1974 by Macmillan London and by Bradbury Press. For this 1990 Bradbury Press edition, Paul Goble has rewritten the text and created new art for the jacket.

Bradbury Press
An Affiliate of Macmillan, Inc.
866 Third Avenue, New York, NY 10022
Collier Macmillan Canada, Inc.

Printed and bound in the United States of America
First Edition
10 9 8 7 6 5 4 3 2 1

LIBRARY OF CONGRESS CATALOGING-IN-PUBLICATION DATA
Goble, Paul.
    Dream wolf / story and illustrations by Paul Goble.—1st ed.
        p.   cm.
    Rev. ed. of: The friendly wolf. 1st American ed. 1974.
    Summary: When two Plains Indian children become lost, they are cared for and guided safely home by a friendly wolf.
    ISBN 0-02-736585-9
    1. Indians of North America—Juvenile fiction.   [1. Wolves—Fiction.   2. Indians of North America—Fiction.]   I. Goble, Paul. Friendly wolf.   II. Title.
PZ7.G5384Dr   1990
[E]—dc19   89-687   CIP   AC

In the old days the people travelled over the plains. They followed the great herds of buffalo.

Every year when the berries were ripe, they would leave the plains and go up into the hills. They made camp in a valley where the berry bushes grow. Everyone picked great quantities. They mashed the berries into little cakes which they dried in the sun. These they stored in painted bags for the winter.

Tiblo (tee-blow) was too young to play with the older boys. He and his little sister, Tanksi (tawnk-she), had to go berry-picking with their mother and the other women and children.

Tiblo was soon tired of picking, and too full to eat any more. When nobody was looking he slipped away with Tanksi to climb the hills.

They climbed up and up among the rocks and
cedar trees where bighorn sheep and bears live.
Soon they could hardly hear the berry-pickers
laughing and calling to each other far below.
Tiblo wanted to reach the top. They climbed on.

   They never noticed the sun starting to go down
behind the hills.

It was getting dark when Tiblo knew they had to
go back home. In the twilight every hill and valley
looked the same. He did not know which way to go.
He called out. . . . Only the echoes answered him.

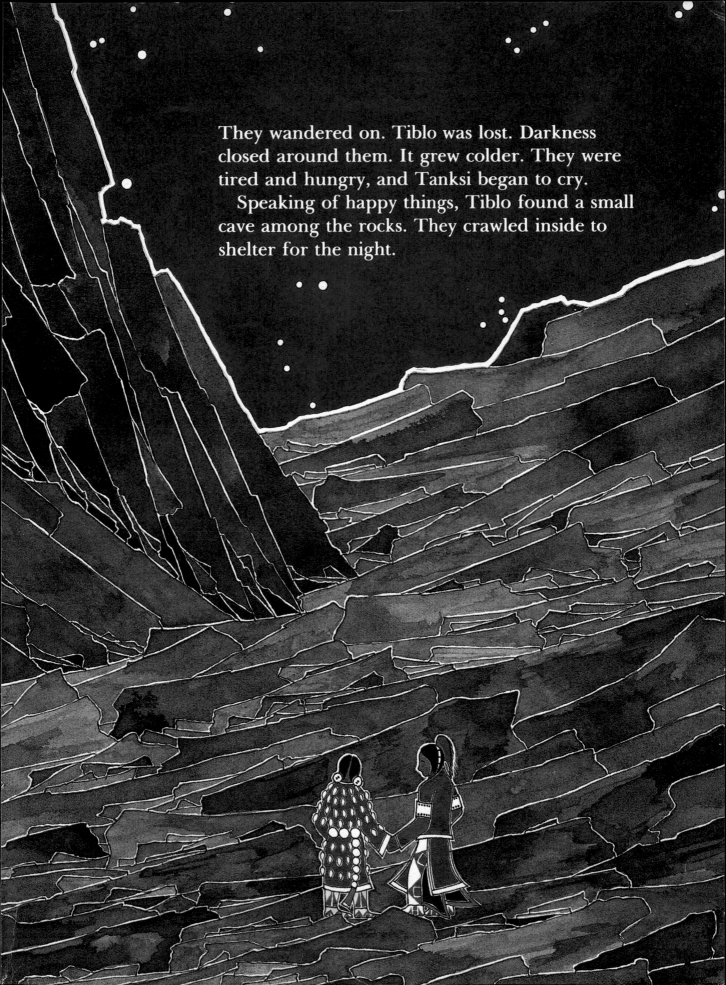

They wandered on. Tiblo was lost. Darkness
closed around them. It grew colder. They were
tired and hungry, and Tanksi began to cry.
  Speaking of happy things, Tiblo found a small
cave among the rocks. They crawled inside to
shelter for the night.

The children were tired, and in a little while they fell asleep. Tiblo had a dream.

He dreamed that a wolf with shining eyes entered the cave. In his dream he felt the wolf's hot breath and its rough tongue licking his face. The wolf lay down beside him. His shaggy fur was like a blanket which kept Tiblo and Tanksi warm.

The sun was already shining into the mouth of the cave when Tiblo opened his eyes again.

Tiblo woke up his sister. They crawled out of the
cave into the warm sunshine. He took Tanksi by
the hand, and they set off walking down the hill.

When the children came to a stream, they
stopped to drink. Suddenly Tiblo saw that a
wolf was sitting on some rocks close by, watching
them. At once he remembered his dream.

"O Wolf," Tiblo said, "we are lost. Mother will
be crying. Help us to find our way home again."

The wolf panted and smiled. "My children, do
not worry. I will help you. Last night you slept in
my den. Follow me now, and I will take you home."

The wolf trotted off. He looked back to see that the children were following. From time to time he trotted ahead out of sight, but he always returned.

At last the wolf led them to a hilltop. The children were filled with joy to see their home in the valley below. The wolf sat back on his haunches and smiled. And then he trotted off back toward the hills. The children begged him to come and live with them.

"No," the wolf called back, "I like to wander from place to place with my friends. Listen for me in the evenings! You will hear me calling, and you will know that I never forget you."

People in the camp saw the children coming down the hill. The men jumped on to their horses, and galloped out to bring them home. Everyone was happy that the children were safe.

Tiblo told how the wolf had brought them home.
Everyone walked into the hills to thank the wolf.
They spread a blanket for him to sit on. They
gave him necklaces and other beautiful gifts.

There has been close kinship with the Wolf
People for as long as anyone can remember.
That is what they say.

The wolves are no longer heard calling in the
evenings at berry-picking time. Hunters have
killed and driven them away with guns and traps
and poisons. People say that the wolves will
return when we, like Tiblo and Tanksi, have the
wolves in our hearts and dreams again.

Young men travelling to capture horses from their enemies heard an old wolf singing this advice:

1. At daybreak
   I roam,
   Running
   I roam.

2. At daybreak
   I roam,
   Trotting
   I roam.

3. At daybreak
   I roam,
   Timidly
   I roam.

4. At daybreak
   I roam,
   Watching cautiously
   I roam.

A man dreamed that he heard wolf puppies singing inside their den. They seemed to tell him: "We are left here helpless, but our parents will soon return."

Father is coming home
Howling—
Mother is coming home
Howling—
Father brings us food
And Mother returns home now
Howling—
In a sacred way
Howling—

Walking the vastness of the Great Plains, people felt they were like the wandering wolves. They sang "wolf songs" to strengthen themselves:

I thought I was a wolf
But having eaten nothing
I can scarcely stand.

I thought I was a wolf
But the owls are hooting
And I fear the night.

Some names of people who feel their relationship with the wolves:

Singing Wolf; Hankering Wolf; Wolf Coming Out;
Wolf Walking Alone; Wolf Robe; Wolf Looking Back;
Blind Wolf; Wolf Lying Down; Wolf on the Hill;
Wrinkled Wolf; Mad-Hearted Wolf; Starving Wolf;
Wolf Voice; Wolf Tooth; Wolf Face.